D0608509

He was a scientist in Montreal but soon returned to France to work with people, instead of computers. Theo has now worked in children's television in the UK, France, Germany and Spain for more than ten years and explains, "I have got my head in the clouds, but my feet on the ground."

Delighted with the success of his first book, *Oscar and Hoo*, he says, "I'm now on cloud nine since so many daydreamers have found us!"

MICHAEL DUDOK DE WIT was born in Holland in 1953.

After school Michael studied etching in Geneva and animation in the UK, where he made his first film, *The Interview*.

As well as illustrating books, he teaches animation, and has directed and animated many award-winning commercials for television and cinema.

Michael's other short animated films include *The Monk and the Fish*, which won numerous prizes and was nominated for an Oscar at the Academy Awards, and *Tom Sweep*. His latest film, *Father and Daughter*, won both an Oscar and a BAFTA award.

To Marcousin and all its friends,
special thanks to Sue, Alison and Sally in London,
Pierre Marchand and his team in Paris, T.

To Arielle, M. D. d. W.

First published in hardback in Great Britain by HarperCollins Children's Books in 2004
First published in paperback in 2005

1 3 5 7 9 10 8 6 4 2

ISBN: 0-00-714009-6

HarperCollins Children's Books is a division of HarperCollins Publishers Ltd.

Text copyright © Theo 2004
Illustrations copyright © Michael Dudok de Wit 2004

The author and illustrator assert the moral right to be identified as the author and illustrator of the work.
A CIP catalogue record for this title is available from the British Library.

Visit our website at: www.harpercollinschildrensbooks.co.uk

Printed and bound in China

Oscar and Hoo Forever

WRITTEN BY **THEO**

ILLUSTRATED BY **MICHAEL DUDOK DE WIT**

HarperCollins *Children's Books*

It's Monday morning and Oscar is daydreaming as usual.

He is on his way to school with his secret friend, Hoo, the little cloud.

Hoo has got something really important to tell Oscar.

"Listen, Oscar..." says Hoo.

But before he can say any more...

"YOO-HOO! OSCAR! HEAD-IN-THE-CLOUDS!"

Oh, no! It's the gang out to make trouble again.

Hoo whirls into action.

"Hey," yell the bullies. "It's gone all dark!"

Oscar and Hoo
slip away laughing.
"I'm glad I've got a friend
like you!" says Oscar.

Later, Oscar is in the classroom and sees that
Hoo is trying to tell him something.
Something important.

At break time, Oscar looks for Hoo.

"Hoo!" he calls. "Where are you?"

At last he spots a damp little wisp floating in a corner.

"What's the matter, Hoo?" asks Oscar.

"I'm homesick," whispers Hoo with a windy little sigh.

Poor Hoo is missing his cloud flock very badly

and he is shrinking in despair.

Even after school, Hoo keeps shrinking.
Oscar is very worried. He doesn't
want his supper and he won't
even watch TV. By bedtime,
Hoo has almost disappeared.

"Bath time!" calls Oscar's mum.

That's when Oscar has an idea.

Perhaps there is a way to

help his friend!

Oscar takes tiny little Hoo
into the bathroom and...Yes!
In the warm steam
Hoo starts to grow...

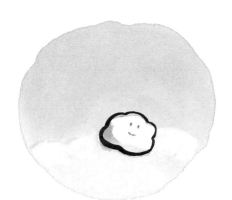

...and grow and grow.

And when Oscar tickles him,
Hoo explodes in a thundery laugh,
"Oscar, you are my very best friend!"

That night, Oscar and Hoo

have a long talk. Oscar knows that the little cloud

must find his flock or he will get sick again.

"But I don't want to leave you," sighs Hoo. "What can we do?"

"There's one place we can find your flock together," answers

Oscar. "In our dreams! Where everything is possible."

"But clouds can't dream," says Hoo.

"Then I'll dream a dream big enough for
both of us!" says Oscar.

"Will we find my flock in your dream?"

"We'll try. Just close your eyes..."

Oscar is dreaming he can fly. And Hoo is with him!

"Your dream is as big as my sky," cries Hoo.

"You cloudy little clown!" says Oscar,
"I'll catch you!"

On they fly, over vast mountain ranges, capped with snow.

"I love mountains," giggles Hoo. "They tickle my tummy."

Below them, the towns and villages unroll like

a map and the people are no bigger than

tiny fleas, hopping about.

Oscar and Hoo fly through a dark forest...

...and then they come to the open sea.

"This is wonderful!" sighs Oscar happily.

"But where's my flock?" says Hoo.

Before Oscar can answer, heavy storm clouds slowly surround them like huge, grey giants.

Oscar hides behind Hoo.

"What's happening?" he gasps.

CRACK!

Lightning shoots
across the sky.
"Help!" shouts Oscar.

"Don't be scared," says
Hoo, puffing himself up.
"Look who's coming...

It's my flock! They've found us."
Together, Hoo and his flock show Oscar how
to chase away the storm clouds.

At last the sky is bright again.

"Oscar," laughs Hoo. "Say hello to the best clouds in the sky."

All of a sudden...

"Oscar!"

calls his mum
from downstairs.
"Time to get up!"

Oscar opens his eyes.
"I've had such a lovely dream,
Hoo," he yawns. "I dreamed we
found your flock and played
chase with the storm clouds –"
"But I dreamed that too!"
cries Hoo.

"Oscar," says Hoo as they hurry to school. "I've got

something important to tell you. I don't have to leave you.

We can play cloud games with my flock every night."

"And we'll share our dreams," laughs Oscar,

"FOREVER!"

Who would you like to find in your dreams?

Just close your eyes...